Dear Parents:

Congratulations! Your child is taking the first steps on an exciting journey. The destination? Independent reading!

STEP INTO READING® will help your child get there. The program offers five steps to reading success. Each step includes fun stories and colorful art or photographs. In addition to original fiction and books with favorite characters, there are Step into Reading Non-Fiction Readers, Phonics Readers and Boxed Sets, Sticker Readers, and Comic Readers—a complete literacy program with something to interest every child.

Learning to Read, Step by Step!

Ready to Read   Preschool–Kindergarten
• big type and easy words • rhyme and rhythm • picture clues
For children who know the alphabet and are eager to begin reading.

Reading with Help   Preschool–Grade 1
• basic vocabulary • short sentences • simple stories
For children who recognize familiar words and sound out new words with help.

Reading on Your Own   Grades 1–3
• engaging characters • easy-to-follow plots • popular topics
For children who are ready to read on their own.

Reading Paragraphs   Grades 2–3
• challenging vocabulary • short paragraphs • exciting stories
For newly independent readers who read simple sentences with confidence.

Ready for Chapters   Grades 2–4
• chapters • longer paragraphs • full-color art
For children who want to take the plunge into chapter books but still like colorful pictures.

STEP INTO READING® is designed to give every child a successful reading experience. The grade levels are only guides; children will progress through the steps at their own speed, developing confidence in their reading.

Remember, a lifetime love of reading starts with a single step!

Published in the United States by Random House Children's Books, a division of Penguin Random House LLC, 1745 Broadway, New York, NY 10019, and in Canada by Penguin Random House Canada Limited, Toronto.

Step into Reading, Random House, and the Random House colophon are registered trademarks of Penguin Random House LLC.

Visit us on the Web!
StepIntoReading.com
rhcbooks.com

Educators and librarians, for a variety of teaching tools, visit us at RHTeachersLibrarians.com

ISBN 978-0-593-64682-3 (trade) — ISBN 978-0-593-64683-0 (lib. bdg.)

Printed in the United States of America
10 9 8 7 6 5 4 3 2 1

nickelodeon

TEENAGE MUTANT NINJA TURTLES MUTANT MAYHEM

MEET THE MUTANTS!

by Matt Huntley
illustrated by Erik Doescher
based on the screenplay by Seth Rogen & Evan Goldberg &
Jeff Rowe, and Dan Hernandez & Benji Samit

Random House 🏠 New York

Baxter Stockman is
a scientist.

He makes a powerful
green ooze.

Oh no!
The ooze spills
into the sewer!

6

It changes four
baby turtles.
They become mutants!

The turtles grow up.

They become the Teenage Mutant Ninja Turtles!

Leonardo is the leader.

He makes the plans.

Raphael is strong.

He is ready to rumble!

Michelangelo is funny.

He likes to tell jokes.

Donatello is
super smart.
He builds all
the Turtles' gear.

Splinter is also

a mutant.

He is a very wise rat.

He teaches the Turtles
their ninja skills.

Some mutants are bad.
Superfly is the boss
of a mutant gang.

Leatherhead is a mutant
crocodile.

She is big and mean.

Bebop is a
mutant warthog.

Rocksteady is a
mutant rhino.
They are both tough,
strong, and ready
to battle.

Mondo Gecko is a
cool dude.

He likes to skateboard!

The ooze changed
a manta ray
into Ray Fillet.
He is one fishy guy!

Genghis Frog is
always happy to hop
into action.

What is flying through
the night sky?
Wingnut is a mutant bat.

Who can stop
these bad mutants?
The Teenage Mutant
Ninja Turtles will
save the day!